S0-DVE-153

PRAISE FOR BROKEN BANNERS
A REAPER OF STONE BOOK 2

"[A] short epic, full of hope and victory where none can be found... The world these authors created is unbelievably tangible."

— *Twin Reads*

"I was in need of a book I could completely lose myself in and this... was the perfect remedy."

— *Paein & Ms4Tune*

"*Broken Banners* is an example of writing fantasy done to perfection."

— *Books for the Beach*

PRAISE FOR A REAPER OF STONE

"Gelineau and King have created a multi-layered world which resounds with... traditional fantasy yet unfolds in the fast-paced and action-filled narrative which we've come to expect... [they] have fashioned a universe I would wish to return to time and time again."

— *Books by Proxy*

"A classic fantasy tale with a strong, admirable heroine and a nice emotional punch. Great start to an enjoyable new series!"

— RL King, author of *The Alastair Stone Chronicles*

"[T]he myths and legends are tangible and the world's history lingers just beneath the surface of the storyline. I loved the resolution."

— *Galleywampus*

PRAISE FOR REND THE DARK

"Atmospheric, fast paced, engaging quick read, with a satisfying story and glimpses of *Supernatural* and King's *IT*. This is definitely a series I can get hooked on and look forward to month after month."

— *BooksChatter*

"*Rend the Dark* really is a good old fashioned horror adventure with an exciting plot and strong characters that you would root for from beginning to end. Like *A Reaper of Stone*, *Rend the Dark* is very fast paced and has an intriguing story that can really pull you in."

— *White Sky Project*

Wow. This is an awesomely dark and scary world these writers have created. I love their use of runes and tattoos. Children with Sight and adults who no longer believe. It's a world I will enjoy visiting, for certain.

— *Paranormal Romance and Authors that Rock*

PRAISE FOR BEST LEFT IN THE SHADOWS

"I was blown away by the detail and world building that was accomplished in so few pages. I didn't feel like I was seeing a section of a puzzle, more like I was reading a story that would contribute to a larger whole, but is compelling and rich all on its own."

— *Mama Reads, Hazel Sleeps*

"Like with the previous *Ascended* books, I really love the characters and their dynamic. The female lead Alys is different from the heroines in *Reaper* and *Rend the Dark*, but she's just as complex and strong."

— *White Sky Project*

PRAISE FOR FAITH AND MOONLIGHT

"*Faith and Moonlight* is reminiscent of Terry Pratchett in that laced through the heavy atmosphere, array of emotion, and implausible magic is hope. That spirit of what might be lightens the feel considerably, making for a delightful story."

– Rabid Readers Reviews

"Amazing, well-developed, and relatable characters combines with snappy, realistic dialogue and simple prose to make this coming of age story… a true fantasy gem."

– Cover2Cover

"A heartbreaking narrative that was so realistic at times, I forgot I was reading fantasy."

– Mama Reads, Hazel Sleeps

"You can really feel Roan's desire and dream to be something more and you can also feel Kay's frustration and struggle. And underneath all that you can practically touch how much they care about each other."

– White Sky Project

MARK GELINEAU
JOE KING

BROKEN
BANNERS

AN ECHO OF THE ASCENDED

Copyright © 2016 by Mark Gelineau and Joe King

All rights reserved.

No part of this book may be reproduced in any form or by any electronic or mechanical means including information storage and retrieval systems, without permission in writing from the author. The only exception is by a reviewer, who may quote short excerpts in a review.

This book is a work of fiction. Names, characters, places, and incidents either are products of the author's imagination or are used fictitiously. Any resemblance to actual persons, living or dead, events, or locales is entirely coincidental. Printed in the United States of America.

First Printing: February 2016

v1.2

Gelineau and King

ISBN 978-1-944015-09-1

www.gelineauandking.com

.

ALDIS

Lieutenant Aldis Janen frowned as his opponent raised his blade in a crisp salute from across the dueling circle. The salute was much too sharp for a man with a large dose of poison running through him.

Damn, Aldis thought.

What had looked to be a promising day had just taken a decisive step in the opposite direction.

It had to be the bastard's weight. Lieutenant Garm Crispin had put on considerable girth in his time leading the Forty-Second. *Soft living at the feet of the warden, no doubt*, Aldis thought bitterly. That extra weight had obviously been enough to slow the poison Aldis had sneaked into his wine.

Or perhaps what he bought was not poison at all. That old crone had likely given him nothing but water in that vial.

The thought rankled him.

Aldis hated being cheated.

And now, when the moron should have been shaking and wobbling, he was instead holding his blade high, waiting for Aldis to return the salute.

Loud jeers and catcalls sounded from the soldiers around them. All wore the king's black and silver, just like Aldis and his opponent, but half sported the tan markings of the Forty-Second, while the rest bore the green of the Ninety-Fifth Pioneers, the unit Aldis commanded.

His soldiers were watching. Best not to disappoint them.

Aldis hadn't actually wanted to have to fight this duel, but it didn't mean he couldn't win. All he had to do was mark the fat bastard. Bleed him twice and the deed would be done. Then, Aldis could move on with his grand plans. Hell, it wasn't like it was a duel to the death.

Aldis assumed his most confident smile, raised his sword with a flourish, and saluted.

And then things went to hell.

Crispin lumbered forward, swinging his blade like he was felling trees rather than fighting a duel. There was no finesse or grace in his strikes or movements. Aldis moved out of reach of the clumsy swings, but as he did, he saw the other man's brow dripping with sweat and his left eye twitching. His breathing was labored already, despite the duel just starting.

So the old woman had not lied about the poison after all.

But rather than causing Crispin to slow, it seemed to infect him like a fever. The lieutenant lumbered toward Aldis, his eyes wild, white foam frothing on his lips.

Crispin swung his thin blade like an axe and Aldis had to parry to keep it from cleaving his skull. As he did, he bound the sword down, driving the tip into the cobblestones. Then, with no warning, Crispin crumpled onto the blade, snapping it at the hilt with a keening ring.

The crowd grew silent as dark blood pooled beneath the body.

No, Aldis thought. *Oh no!*

A junior officer from the Forty-Second knelt down and felt Crispin's neck. "Dead," the man said.

The circle of soldiers erupted into shouts and threats.

As soon as they did, Aldis's own second-in-command, Sergeant Kyra, rushed to his side. Her loud, brash voice barked by his ear, "Fair fight. All saw it. No blame on the lieutenant if your man couldn't keep from falling on his own damn blade!"

Violence was in the air as surely as the scent of blood. Aldis's first instinct was to run. His second was to fight and see what happened. Neither seemed particularly wise.

Then, the provosts showed up and made the decision easy.

They rolled in with truncheons out, and Aldis ordered his men to run. The assembled soldiers from both units scattered, leaving Aldis alone.

The provosts clapped irons on him and led him away.

How had such a promising day had gone so wrong?

He never should have trusted that grizzled old crone at the apothecary, but he had had to. Warden Rollon needed a crew to deal with a situation, and Aldis wanted that commission. Actually, he needed it. Desperately. His rise in station had cost him, and he owed money to a line of creditors stretching all the way back to Resa.

He had gambled everything on landing the commission. It had been down to his own Ninety-Fifth and Crispin's Forty-Second. That was when he had thought to arrange the duel. A few words here, a little rumor there; just enough to get old Crispin thoroughly heated.

But now? The murder of a fellow officer? The bastard wasn't supposed to die. This would mean prison. Or worse.

The cold iron manacles brought him back to the present and he realized something was wrong. They weren't taking him to the stockade, but rather into the towering central keep.

The hair on the back of Aldis's neck stood on end. Something was up.

After a short walk down a stone hallway, one of the provosts opened the door while the other removed Aldis's manacles.

Aldis stepped inside, half-expecting a knife between his ribs.

Instead, as the door shut behind him, a small light appeared. Someone hidden in shadow pulled back the slide on a lantern, shining light in Aldis's direction. Aldis squinted his eyes, trying to get them to adjust.

The figure behind the lantern spoke and Aldis's stomach clenched with recognition. "And here, I thought you had changed since your more foolish days at the Academy," came the cold, flat voice of Bayun. The man was Warden Rollon's chamberlain, but anyone with a real understanding of politics knew Bayun was Warden Rollon's underhand. Bayun handled the things the warden could not, or should not, be involved in.

"Those days are far behind me," Aldis said, keeping his voice even.

"Is that because there are no blonde, idealistic troublemakers here for you to follow? What was her name? Elaine? Elise?"

Aldis knew enough of the game to know how this was being played. "Elinor," he corrected, fully aware the chamberlain knew all about his past and the people in it. "No. It was more that I realized that path was not conducive to an actual career."

In the dim lantern light, Bayun smiled.

"A career. Do you know what else most people would consider not conducive to a successful career, Lieutenant Janen? Poisoning a fellow officer before a duel that you yourself instigated and then watching the man bleed out like a slaughtered goat on the stones of the lower pavilion."

Hearing his machinations put so bluntly, all hope died in Aldis's heart. He was done. It was simply a matter of whether he would survive prison long enough to dance on the gallows.

"Fortunately for you, Lieutenant, the warden and I are not most people."

Aldis's mouth fell open. "Sir?" he asked, lamely.

Bayun came out from the other side of the table. Though short and with a withered left arm, the man exuded a sense of power and menace. "Lieutenant, the warden has a delicate matter that needs attention. It should be a relatively simple task for one of your…resourceful nature."

As Aldis listened, relief morphed into warm ambition. Not only was he being spared, but he was being offered an opportunity. Warden Rollon and Bayun's favor would elevate him to an entirely new level of power and influence.

The day was definitely shaping up.

***

Aldis could hardly keep the grin from his face. He pushed open the doors to the tavern that had become the second home for the Ninety-Fifth.

"Lieutenant!" one man yelled out almost immediately.

"Thought you was clipped sure, sir," said a short woman with a tankard in her hand.

Hearing his name on the lips of dozens made his grin grow even larger.

"Clipped?" he said with a laugh. "Lieutenant Aldis Janen? Please! I was merely summoned for a very special meeting." He stepped up onto one of the tables, his boots knocking over a flagon of wine. Aldis gestured broadly, commanding the attention of the whole room.

"Brothers and sisters of the Ninety-Fifth. It seems we have ourselves a new set of orders." He pulled forth the signed documents and held them out proudly. "An important job at the behest of Warden Rollon himself! He's sending me to Cragswatch March and I want to know only one thing. Will you follow me there?"

Aldis drank in the cheers like wine.

One soldier came forward. *Sandson*, Aldis thought the man's name was, but there were so many in the unit it was hard to keep them straight. He looked up at Aldis with adulation.

"Sir, can I buy you a drink?" the young man asked.

Aldis jumped down from the table and clapped him on the shoulder. "No," he said, shaking his head dramatically. "But I will buy you one. In fact, I will buy one for every brave man or woman under my command."

The cheers grew louder.

With a tankard in hand, Aldis offered a toast to the crowded room. "To Cragswatch. To the Ninety-Fifth. It's our time now," he said. "Let us show them our quality!"

He drained the cup as soldiers chanted his name.

ELINOR

It was a beautiful morning.

The light snow gave the sharp, craggy peaks a pristine white dressing, gleaming like new gold in the rich glow of morning. Flurries of light danced along the mountainside, sparkling and shifting. They reminded Elinor of old stories of mountain spirits in the time of Aedan; the breath of the mountain as it lay dreaming.

Then, just like that, they were gone.

Elinor's short, blonde hair blew in the cold wind and her black uniform snapped and ruffled behind her. Warmth competed with chill air, making her skin tingle.

Slowly, she smiled.

Since Timberline, things felt different. She felt different.

There, she had met the Shepherd of Tree and Stone, had stood before a spirit of the old age. No myth or fanciful tale, but a powerful force almost beyond her comprehension. And before the Shepherd, she had uttered an oath to save a life.

Everything felt more alive now. More urgent. More real. She felt like she was waking up from a long slumber, and she liked it.

There was the crunch of boots in the snow, the familiar cadence of an old friend. Elinor felt as much as heard the approach of her chief of engineers.

"I did not think it was possible," Elinor said, turning around, "but I can actually hear you frowning, Con."

Journeyman Engineer Conbert Eylnen moved up beside her. "An awful lot to be frowning about, Elinor. I still don't understand why you're taking this so calmly."

"Orders are orders, Con."

"They've stripped us of our entire contingent of engineers," he said. "The lot of them. All to be transferred to the Ninety-Fifth." His frown deepened. "This is punishment for Timberline."

Elinor nodded, though she did not match his frustration. "Yes, it is, but I will not regret the past, Con." She rested a gloved hand on his shoulder. "It will be alright. We've been through bad and worse before."

She clapped him a bit harder on the shoulder, signaling a change in topic. "On the bright side, at least we will see Aldis soon."

Con groaned. "Only in the true depths of our current despair could that be considered a good thing."

"I know he can be a bit brash, but it will do both of us some good to see an old friend." Her smile grew wider. "Despite his faults, I do miss his humor and good spirits."

"Aldis Janen is a spoiled wastrel who has always been able to get by on his charm and his family," he said. "He has never achieved a genuine thing in his life. You've always given him a pass on his character defects because he was kind to you in the Academy."

"Absolutely. When so few others were. I do not forget such things, Con."

He sighed. "I'm just saying that your feelings for him tend to cloud your judgment."

She moved off her rocky perch. "You two never got along."

"No, we most certainly did not."

"Well, then the good news for you is when we see him later today, you will have another chance to mend things, now won't you?" she asked with a smile as she headed back toward the camp.

Elinor took stock of the large wagons being pulled by the mule teams. "With some luck, we can reach Height's Ward Keep, or what's left of it, by nightfall." She pointed to a cliff, a short distance from their position. "We should have a good glimpse of the road from there. Think you're up for a little climb, Journeyman Engineer?"

Con sighed, but followed her up the cliff.

Before long, he was catching his breath. "I don't—I don't know how you do that so fast," he wheezed.

Elinor said nothing. Her eyes focused in the direction of Height's Ward Keep. In the distance, a cloud of dark shapes stained the sky.

Carrion birds.

"Rouse the camp. I want us covering ground in under an hour," Elinor said, moving. "At the hop and weapons to hand. Prepared for trouble."

Con was already scrambling back down, shouting orders to get the company moving.

CON

Con and Elinor rode into a scene of horror.

The large clearing was filled with torn and shattered bodies. Dozens of men and women lay in the snow, their red blood frozen on their black uniforms.

Black uniforms of the King's Army.

"By the First Ascended," Con swore, staring out at the charnel scene before them.

He knelt down beside one of the corpses. The black uniform had a green stripe down the arms; an engineer.

Cold dread curled inside Con's stomach like a sleeping snake. This was the other reclamation group. The Ninety-Fifth Pioneers.

Con moved to another body. A woman's face stared up at him, eyes wide with fear. He recognized her. Her name had been Rina. Rina something. A noble, but he couldn't remember her family name. He had known her in the Academy.

"Elinor, this is the Ninety-Fifth," Con said. "I know—I knew some of these people." He shook his head. "What happened here?"

"All the wounds are to their backs, Con," Elinor said. "They were run down. Taken from behind." She scanned the clearing, her eyes hard. "Where are the rest of them?"

"What do you mean?" Con asked, but even as he said it, he understood. Unlike their contingent, the Ninety-Fifth Pioneers were a full cohort. They traveled with forty soldiers and over twice that in attached engineers and teamsters. There were no more than fifty bodies in the clearing.

Con looked back to Elinor. "Lieutenant Janen?"

"Aldis isn't here," she said.

In her voice, Con heard an equal mix of relief and worry.

She moved across the bloodstained clearing until she stood above a body that clasped a long pole. A torn banner dangled from it.

Elinor removed the banner and folded it silently. With each crisp, precise movement, Con saw tension grow on her face. Cold fury in her eyes.

"What do we do, Elinor?"

"These were soldiers of the King's Army. Our brothers and sisters. We bury them," she said. Then her voice grew colder. "And then we find who did this."

BROKEN BANNERS

ELINOR

Height's Ward Keep stood tall and proud in the distance. Its single, central tower rose like the mast of a ship over the squat, solid construction of its central structure. Its stone walls were dark against the snow-covered hills. It looked powerful and indestructible.

And that was the damn problem.

Aldis's Ninety-Fifth had been assigned to reap it. It should have been taken a month ago, but the keep still stood.

And where was Aldis? For a moment, she imagined him lying dead in a field somewhere, and her stomach tightened. Aldis had a knack for getting into trouble, but he was just as good at getting out of it.

But to leave his men behind like that?

Con rode up beside her. "Nothing makes sense," he said quietly. "Do you think Army Command knew what was happening here when they ordered us out here? Knew that something was wrong?"

"I doubt it," Elinor said. "Those bodies are only a couple days dead. And remember, they didn't send us out here to reinforce Aldis and the Ninety-Fifth. They sent us to transfer."

Elinor gritted her teeth as she stared out from the edge of the forest. In the distance, a small village sat between the forest and the keep.

She pointed down the slope. "Perhaps we will find some answers there," she said. "Leave the engineers here with the wagons and heavy equipment. And get me Edmur."

Con nodded and wheeled his horse around.

Elinor continued her slow approach to the village. Her eyes tracked the movement of villagers moving among the houses.

It was only a few minutes before the foreman for the civilian work crew jogged up beside her horse. He was a sly-looking man with hair cut close to his head and cunning eyes sharp under dark brows.

"Ta, Boss," Edmur said in a thick Lowside accent.

He always called her that and the habit had spread to the rest of the workers in his crew. Few officers of the King's Army would allow such an informal address, but it reminded her of her sister Alys. Actually, she saw a lot of Alys in Edmur. He was smart, unflinching, and efficient, as was his crew.

Elinor recognized Lowside qualities for what they meant.

They were survivors.

"Edmur, I need your crew with me as we go into the village."

"Right, right," he nodded. "I can see that, Boss. But before we take steps down into the lovely ville, you and me have to talk business."

Elinor fixed him with an icy stare. "I can assure you, Edmur, this is absolutely not the time for this."

"Anytime we come across a damn butcher's mess like we done in that clearing, it most definitely is the time," he said. "My lot and I didn't sign up for nothing like that. If we wanted the rough, we would have all stayed Lowside in Resa. I have a responsibility to my crew. See 'em safe and see 'em paid. If I can't vouch for one, I have to vouch for the other."

He gave her a smile that was clearly intended to be charming. "When the rest of the crews scampered off, remember it was me and mine what stayed. But, I've no intention of ending up like those poor bastards back up the road."

"You only stayed because I promised you the wages the other crews forfeited, but you are welcome to take your crew and go at any time," she said. "But you travel alone and after what we saw this morning, I cannot guarantee your safety."

As the words came out of her mouth, Elinor saw something hanging from one of the eaves. It swayed heavily in the cold wind. There were two more shapes suspended from the house opposite.

Bodies. Hanging bodies.

Edmur's eyes went sharp. "Alright. We're in it too deep now. We play it your way, Boss. I'll bring up the boys."

"Just keep them in check, Edmur. There is no trouble yet."

"Is that optimism? Yeah, never had much cause to learn that Lowside."

Elinor ignored him, her focus directed toward the villagers. They were shabby and weak-looking, dark circles of exhaustion juxtaposed against faces angular from hunger. Elinor maneuvered her horse in front of a young man. Even with such a brazen movement, he did not look up.

She sensed fear coming off him like a tangible thing.

"Are you alright?" Elinor asked.

The young man said nothing.

"Where is the headsman for the village?" she asked.

Slowly, without looking up, the young man pointed to the first of the hanging bodies. Con pulled up beside her. His face was ashen.

Then, there were shouts in the streets.

Villagers moved frantically, running into houses, doors slamming shut. The young man ran and Elinor's horse shied away from the sudden movement. As she gripped the reins to steady it, she saw what had prompted the villagers to panic. In the far distance, the heavy gates of the keep were open.

A group of horsemen rode forth.

Elinor pointed back toward the treeline. "Con, get your engineers back into the forest and rig something up to deter those horsemen if they come in after us."

"There's not enough time for anything like that."

"I'll buy you the time," Elinor said. "Go!"

He gave her one last look and then was off.

"Edmur, time to earn that pay. I need you and your men with me in the village. Stay in plain sight. Let those horsemen see you."

"Are you daft? We're heading out of here!"

"Those bodies in the clearing were run down from behind. You stand with me and I will see you through this. You run now and all you will get is a blade to the back from those riders."

Edmur stared at the approaching horsemen. "You'd best be as good as your word, Boss," he said.

As she wheeled her horse around, he shook his head. "Where the hell you going?"

"I'm going to go talk to them," Elinor said, then spurred her horse forward.

There were ten riders coming, all armed. As she drew closer, she raised her arm in salute. "Ho, riders from the keep," she said, coming to a stop.

The lead rider was a tall man. His face was worn and leathery and he had cold, hard eyes that seemed incongruous with the easy smile he wore. "Ho to you, officer. What brings the soldiers of the King's Army here to Height's Ward?"

Her horse shied and danced as she unconsciously tightened her legs against its flanks. Elinor swallowed once, but kept her chin held high as she met the man's eyes. "The deaths of my fellow soldiers," she said, her voice clear and crisp. "In a clearing up the road from your keep lie the bodies of my fallen brothers and sisters and I am here to know why."

The tall man nodded slowly. "A tragedy. We said farewell to the soldiers yesterday, but not long after their departure, we heard the sounds of battle carrying to us. Our lord sent us out to investigate, but we were too late."

He gave a discouraged sigh. "Filthy bandits. We tracked the large force of them heading East, but we could not pursue and leave our lord undefended. When we saw your men approaching the village, in truth, we feared that you were that group come to attack us. At least until we saw your uniform."

Elinor's expression did not change. "You are with Lord Desmond then?"

"Yes, indeed. Great Lord Desmond."

The chill of unease blossomed like ice, spreading through her. Lord Desmond was to be the new lord of this march now that the line of Redmayne had ended. The lord whose transition into power Aldis should have overseen a month ago.

These were not the men of Lord Desmond.

They were rough looking. Their leathers and bits of armor were worn and dull. Her eyes flashed to the distant keep and, even from here, she saw a banner flying from the tower. It looked ragged and worn. A sight no lord would ever allow.

She hoped Con was making good use of this time.

"I would pay my respects to your lord," Elinor said, "but justice for forty-seven of the King's Own cannot be put off. The bandits headed east, you say? Very well. We will seek them there." She turned her horse and began to trot back toward the village.

As she did, she heard the tell-tale whispering sound of blades being drawn. It seemed she was as poor a liar as he was. At the sound, she kicked her horse hard in the flanks and shot forward, racing across the snow. Behind her, the riders rode hard in pursuit.

Elinor bent low over the neck of her horse, urging him to greater speed. Small houses of the village flew past and she saw Edmur up ahead, a few of his men by his side.

"Run!" she yelled.

They scrambled up the short path and disappeared into the trees. Behind her, she heard her pursuers, the beating hooves of their horses pounding like drums.

Elinor entered the forest, long branches scraping her as she raced past. She pushed further and faster, her heart pounding in her chest.

"Now!" she heard Con's voice yell before something twanged with a high-pitched vibration. Strangled cries and panicked shrieks rang out behind her.

Elinor turned around just as the second wave of riders hit the length of rope at their chest, throwing them violently from their horses. The first riders were already on the ground and these others fell heavily atop their fellows, man and beast alike crying out in the chaos.

Edmur and his work crew were already on the downed riders. They swung shovels and small blades, and the confused screams of the men on the ground were short-lived.

"Do not let them escape!" Elinor yelled out.

A flash of movement caught her attention. It was the tall rider, the leader of the group. He was barely a few strides away, gazing back in shock. He met her gaze with a look of fear and hatred, but then turned his horse and raced toward the village.

Elinor followed, weaving through the trees to catch him. "Stand down!" she yelled at the rider. "Stand and you will be spared. I give you my word."

As she bore down on him, he swung wildly with his sword. She easily leaned out of the way and the sharp edge whistled harmlessly past her. The rider raised his blade high, standing tall in the saddle. As he did, a low branch caught him and threw him from his mount in a whirling cartwheel. She heard a sickening crunch.

He lay in a broken slump on the forest floor, his eyes staring wide and lifeless.

There would be no answers from him.

Elinor gritted her teeth and made her way to the road. She caught sight of Con, his familiar black uniform dirty with leaves. In one hand, he held his officer's blade and, in the other, a huge iron hook.

"Elinor," Con said, relief clear in his voice.

"You do impressive work quickly, Chief Engineer," she said, giving him a grateful smile.

"With more time, I could have built a ballista," Con said, coming up to take the reins of her horse.

Absently, Elinor nodded, her mind already at work. "You may still need to. Someone has taken Height's Ward Keep."

ELINOR

There was something sad and broken about the state of the village. The buildings were well made, with a craftsman's attention to detail. Intricate carvings of small flowers and birds were cut into the support posts for one of the houses. These people had cared for their homes once. Loved them.

That was at odds with what Elinor saw now. Broken shutters were left unrepaired, with only worn blankets nailed up to keep out the winter draft. The rooftops had no fresh tar or thatch. The entire place looked worn down and forgotten.

As she and Con crossed under the shadow of the swinging corpses, she stopped and stared up, her anger growing. Without thinking, she walked to the rope and gently lowered the body. As it came to rest, she covered it with an old horse blanket drying on a fence.

She took down the other bodies as well. Frightened faces looked on from the various doorways. When she had finished, all but one of the doorways had closed. Elinor nodded to Con and headed for it.

A young man in the doorway moved aside. "Come in," he said.

"No!" came a harsh whisper from deeper inside the darkened room. "No, Oltan. You mustn't!"

"Enough, Mother," Oltan whispered back. "These are the soldiers of the king."

Elinor saw an older woman come forward, wrapped in a thick shawl. A large kitchen knife was clenched in her hand. She eyed Elinor and Con with desperate fear. "So was the last group," she said bitterly.

Elinor stepped inside the small house with Con close behind. She moved cautiously to the side of the room, careful to keep Oltan and his mother fully in her vision.

"I saw you outrun the riders. Lead them into the forest," Oltan said, raising his chin. "Did you kill them?"

Elinor nodded.

"Good," the young man said. The bitter vehemence caught Elinor off guard.

Oltan's mother shook her head. "You cannot be here," she said quietly, almost as if mumbling the words to herself. "The lord cannot find you here. He will be angry."

Oltan spun toward her. "He is not our lord, Mother! And I will not bow to that man. Not after what he did to Father." Tears filled the young man's eyes as he spoke.

"My name is Elinor. I am a lieutenant in the King's Army. If I or my men can help you, we will do so." She kept her voice even and spoke slowly. "What has happened here?"

"What has happened?" Oltan laughed bitterly. "Garett returned to claim his birthright, that's what happened."

Behind him, his mother looked around like a cornered animal, as if the name itself might conjure danger into her house.

Con's brows furrowed. "What birthright? The Redmayne line was ended. That is why the Ninety-Fifth was sent here."

"There was no heir," Oltan said. "No rightful heir, at least. Garett was second son. He was gone from Cragswatch for years. Lord Redmayne cast him out."

"Why?" asked Elinor.

The old woman shook her head. "His older brother died. There were dark rumors. It was said Garett killed him. Lord Redmayne banished him from Cragswatch."

Oltan moved over to stand beside his mother. His demeanor toward her softened and he put an arm around her small, bony shoulders.

"When our lord grew sick, the warden appointed Lord Desmond to reclaim the land," Oltan began, his voice rough. "But Garett returned. He came at the head of a force of thugs and bandits. And once the old lord died, Garett asserted that he was entitled to our land by virtue of blood."

The young man took a deep breath and choked back tears. "My father knew the final wishes of his rightful lord. He challenged Garett's right." He took deep, shuddering breaths. "And Garett hung him at the edge of the village."

Cold anger and grief blossomed in Elinor's heart. "I am sorry," she said through clenched teeth. She paused a moment out of respect, but then pressed on. "And what of the king's soldiers?"

"The King's Reaper came with his group a month ago," Oltan said. "They set up their wagons around the keep, but did nothing beyond that. I do not know what he was doing up in the keep all that time, but he never came here.

"Two days ago, Lord Desmond arrived to claim the march. That night, the reaper and his men fled. They left their wagons and equipment behind, but they didn't get far. Garett's horsemen caught them in the clearing." He was quiet for a long moment. "Lord Desmond and his entourage never left."

"This is impossible," Elinor said. "Something like this is too hard to keep a secret. You can't just steal a march. The warden would know."

"The warden does know," Oltan said. "Little happens in his domain without his notice. He just doesn't care. So long as the tithes keep coming and gold flows to his coffers, he doesn't bother with us.

He sits in his castle like a king and only his tax collectors and enforcers come to Cragswatch. And neither ever mean good things."

Elinor had heard rumors of Warden Rollon's greed, but what had occurred here at Cragswatch, what had befallen the Ninety-Fifth, had to be something even he could not stand for.

She leaned forward. "Oltan, we've seen the bodies in the clearing, but there are many soldiers unaccounted for. Do you have any idea if there are survivors?"

Oltan shook his head.

Disappointment flared in Elinor's heart, but she pushed it down. "Inside the keep, do you know how many men he has?"

"Many," the young man said. "More than a hundred, I know that much. But worse than that, the old lord's lead Razors turned their coat and sided with Garett. Kala, and that hulking brute, Runcen. They now sit at the side of that bastard, enforcing his will."

She heard Con swear under his breath. Every word Oltan said painted a darker picture. Over a hundred men. All likely hardened fighters from a life of banditry. And two Razors, as well. All told, it was far more than Elinor and her small force could deal with.

She exhaled slowly, forcing herself to focus on the issues at hand. "Right now, the only thing that is keeping us alive is that Garett just lost ten horsemen in that forest and he has no idea the size of the force that took them. That means, for now, he feels a damn sight safer behind the stone of that keep than outside of it."

Con nodded once more.

"Gather everyone up, Con. Let them know what has happened here and tell them to keep doing what they can to make our forces look as sizable as possible. The moment Garett thinks he can take us in a fight on the field, those gates will open and we'll all die here."

"What are you going to do?" Con asked, a worried frown on his face.

"I'm going to buy us some time."

***

Elinor mounted her horse, her blue eyes cold and hard beneath her helm. A cart was hitched behind her with the bodies of the fallen horsemen stacked within it.

She secured a shield to her arm and then slowly unwrapped the banner of the Ninety-Fifth Pioneer Cohort. The fabric was smooth against her hands despite the ragged tears and bloodstains. She held it up in one arm. The wind caught the once-proud ensign and made it snap and dance.

Con stared at her regalia and shook his head. "This is insane," he said in a low voice. "Even for you."

"If this doesn't work, you know what to do."

Con nodded grimly.

Elinor gave a final nod before kicking her horse in the flanks and heading out of the forest. The wagon rattled behind her.

The distance yawned like a chasm of snowy white as Elinor guided her horse forward. In the space between the village and the keep, the isolation of the moment crept in upon her, but she carried herself tall, banner in one hand, shield in the other.

She would show no weakness.

Nearing the structure, Elinor saw the rough faces of archers manning the ramparts. Their expressions showed surprise and confusion. None fired upon her. Their hesitation showed they were afraid and that thought bolstered her.

She reined in her horse and held the banner high. "In the name of Aymeric Vere, King of Aedaron and Scion of the Blood of the First Ascended, I call for Garett, once son of Redmayne."

She held still, watching the men on the battlements. There was a small flurry of activity before a new figure appeared. His clean-shaven face was thin and angular, but his eyes were shadowed and sunken.

"I am Lord Redmayne," he said, emphasizing the title in his response.

It was an emphasis that Elinor pointedly chose to ignore. "Garett, you stand accused of the murder of the king's soldiers and the occupation of a fortress under arms. These crimes constitute treason." Her voice was clear and powerful. "You further stand accused of the murder of Lord Desmond, rightful ruler of this land—"

"I am the rightful ruler of this land," Garett interrupted. His clipped words and raised voice indicated that she had hit a nerve.

He had a temper. Good. She could use that against him.

"You killed a lord and you have attacked the King's Army. You are nothing but a criminal. It will be up to Warden Rollon to decide your ultimate fate. If you surrender yourself and release whatever hostages you may be holding, I guarantee you safe passage to face your judgement."

Garett's sunken eyes bulged. "Who the hell do you think you are, soldier?"

She glared, skewering him with her eyes. "I am Lieutenant Elinor of the King's Army."

At the mention of her name, she heard some whispered words drift down from the battlement. Timberline was mentioned more than once and she allowed her lips to pull back in a smile. Perhaps there was some use to having a reputation.

Quick to capitalize on the moment, Elinor dismounted and unhitched the cart. "I came to return your property." With that, she pulled the tarp off, exposing the bodies of the horsemen. "If you come at me again, I will return all of your men the same way. You have until dawn to submit yourself to the king's justice." She paused, allowing her cold gaze to move across the battlement till they found Garett. "Or you shall answer to mine."

With that, she remounted and rode back toward the village.

Not a single arrow came at her back.

ALDIS

Aldis felt the weight of their stares crushing him. Worse than the stone of the walls. Worse than the cold iron of the bars. The cold condemnation of the surviving members of the Ninety-Fifth made him feel like a trapped animal. If chewing his own leg off would have served to get him out of this cage, he would have gladly bitten in.

Aldis sat alone by the door. Sergeant Kyra moved from the side of one of the injured men and sat beside him.

"Timmon's arm is bad," she said in a low voice. Aldis noticed she did not call him *sir* anymore. "Got the rot in the wound. He needs to lose it or it will kill him."

Aldis shrugged helplessly. "There is nothing we can do for him in here, Kyra. I'm no chiurgeon."

Her eyes did not waver, boring into him. "You still needed to know," she said, her voice flat and cold.

He looked away first.

As he did, the heavy, reinforced door opened and four rough-looking men entered with blades drawn.

The lead one pointed directly at Aldis. "That one. Bring him to Garett," he said.

Aldis got to his feet. "I represent the Ninety-Fifth. I will go to speak with Lord Garett, and gladly." He looked back at Kyra and gave her a nod. "It is alright, Sergeant. I will see to securing the terms of our release." He offered his most confident, charming smile to his broken soldiers. "Wait but a few moments, brothers and sisters. I shall return soon."

There was no response from his men. A few even turned their heads away. As the guards led him away, this time there were no cheers for him. The only sound was the dull clang of the cell door behind him.

Walking into the great hall of the keep, the first thing Aldis noticed was there was still blood on the floor. Even two days after Lord Desmond and his entourage were slaughtered, the blood remained, black and tacky on the cold stone.

At the head of the room, upon a seat that was more chair than throne, Garett Redmayne was busy draining a large tankard. He looked haggard, his eyes sunken and dark. It appeared he had not slept in the days since he murdered Lord Desmond.

Behind him, Aldis saw Garett's two pet Razors: Kala, the woman with knives and the cruel smile, and Runcen, that big bastard with his terrible hammer. They led the force that had pursued him in his hasty escape attempt and were the first to cut into his soldiers.

Garett tipped his tankard upside down to empty it fully and then threw it hard against the stone wall, shattering the crockery into pieces. All around his seat, empty bottles and barrels littered the floor. Clearly there had been quite the celebration, but something had happened.

Aldis watched the man's twitchy movements and wild eyes.

Something scared Garett.

That meant he would be even more dangerous now. More volatile, if such a thing was even possible.

If Aldis was smart, there might be an opportunity here.

And this time, Aldis intended to be very smart.

Garett looked up. "You! What the hell took you so long to get here?"

Aldis allowed an easy smile to cross his face. "I came as soon as I was allowed, my lord," Aldis said, emphasizing the title, knowing Garett liked that. "But I would be happy to serve you in any capacity you have need of."

Kala laughed. "Like the service you offered when you broke faith and tried to run back to the warden?" Her eyes locked onto Aldis. She looked as if she was barely restraining herself from leaping across the space between them and carving him with the knives at her belt.

"A momentary and terrible lapse in judgment, my lord," he said. "One that I assure you will not happen again."

"Not enough men left to try?" Kala said.

Garett stood. "Enough! We don't have time for this," he snapped. "An entire regiment of the King's Army is camped outside my walls!"

That caught Aldis off guard. A regiment? Here? That was impossible. The warden, not wanting to involve himself further, wouldn't bother to send reinforcements and Army Command had no knowledge of what was happening. Nobody should be in the area except—

Realization hit Aldis like cold water to the face.

As if to confirm his conclusion, Garett continued on, "And they are commanded by that mad woman who tore Timberline apart. Elinor."

The name echoed off the stone walls.

Aldis tried to bury his own reaction to the name and focus on Garett's fear. There was still a chance for Aldis to save himself, but he had to be careful. Elinor didn't command a regiment. In fact, she had no infantry under her banner, and her corps of engineers was set to be reassigned to his command. She had to be bluffing Garett somehow.

Aldis ground his teeth in frustration.

By the Ascended, Elinor was here. She was in over her head now, and it was because of him. Aldis let the smile slip from his face.

"I see you know of her reputation," Garett said.

Kala snorted. "To hell with her reputation. I say we ride out and put her to the blade."

"Like Ephed and his ten Razors tried back in Timberline?" Aldis asked. "She put them down easily enough." He tilted his head and looked toward Kala's neck. "He bore a Victory Kiss and held first rank when he fought in the grand tournament. I don't see that mark on you, Razor, and unless your quiet friend there," Aldis said, gesturing toward the massive Runcen, "has nine brothers hiding in here, I'd say you'd hardly make Elinor break a sweat."

There was a feeling of pressure in the room as Kala, eyes flashing in rage, began to tap into her Razor power. Aldis held his breath, knowing exactly the dangerous line he was treading right now.

"Enough, I said!" Garett screamed out, his face flushed from anger and drink. "I am Lord of Cragswatch and I will be obeyed!"

Aldis immediately dropped to one knee. "Apologies, Lord. This is truly a dire situation, but you are fortunate this day. I know Elinor well. We attended the Academy together. We were, and remain, the greatest of friends."

"He's lying," Kala said.

"On my honor," Aldis said. "Allow me to parley with her. I can convince her to lift the siege of Height's Ward Keep and return to the warden. I am sure we can come up with a new arrangement with Warden Rollon. One that will ensure the safety and prosperity of all involved."

Kala leaned toward Garett. "Do not believe this snake. He lies. He has already committed treason."

Aldis laughed bitterly. "Yes, I did commit treason. By performing the very acts that put your lord in power, Razor. I have no value to you at all for ransom or hostage, but I could still serve you as negotiator."

His confident smile returned. "You gambled on me once, Dread Lord. It earned you this keep and your ancestral lands. I ask that you gamble once more, and I will help you keep them."

Garett was silent for a moment, his fingers tapping rapidly on the wooden arm of the chair. "Get her to lift the siege. Get her out of my lands," he said finally.

"With pleasure, Lord," Aldis said with a bow before turning.

He felt Kala's hateful gaze on his back. Let her fume, he thought. He'd never see her again.

As his escorts walked him to the gates, Aldis took stock of the number of men Garett had at his disposal. There were bandits everywhere in the keep. Elinor and her engineers were no match for this many.

The main gate opened and a spear at his back urged him forward. Aldis Janen did not look back as he walked into the snow.

As he crossed the expanse, he heard calls from the village. Aldis extended his arms, showing he was unarmed.

At the outskirts of the village, a small group of figures assembled in the central street, awaiting him. And there she was, tall and proud. Her white-blonde hair mingled with the surrounding snow.

Damn, she was beautiful.

Elinor's face was set and her eyes tracked his every move, but his hood was up against the cold and snow and she could not see his face.

He walked the final stretch and stood in the street before them. Then slowly, he raised his hands and pulled back his hood.

Shock and relief registered on her face. "Aldis?" Elinor said.

Aldis smiled. "Hello, Ellie."

ELINOR

Elinor embraced him fiercely, tears dripping onto his uniform.

There had been a time when Aldis Janen had seemed larger than life. Dashing, confident, handsome, and, perhaps most surprisingly, kind. He had been her friend through some of the hardest, darkest days of the Academy.

For a short time, she even believed she loved him, though he'd never felt the same toward her. After graduation, when they had gone their separate ways, she convinced herself it was only a school girl's crush. Seeing him again brought back old emotions and, after fearing the worst, holding him in her arms made her heart swell.

"You're alive," she said, finally pulling back.

"Yes, thanks to you."

"How did you get out of the keep?"

"I convinced Garett that I knew you and that I could negotiate with you on his behalf." He gave her that familiar, curving smile she remembered so well, but there was something brittle to it now. It lacked the same hallmark dash and daring.

"Negotiate? For what? What terms could he possibly be seeking?"

Aldis leaned forward, his green eyes catching the light from the lanterns hung around them. "That I would get you to lift your siege and return to Warden Rollon."

Hearing his words, Elinor almost laughed. "Then come the morning, he will be relieved. We are already leaving, Aldis."

He blinked and seemed to draw himself up in surprise. "You're leaving?"

"We have reports of a hundred horsemen inside," she said.

"Closer to one hundred twenty and two Razors," he amended. "Yes. Good. Let's get to Warden Rollon. We will be safe there."

Con spoke up, his words clipped and sharp. "What happened, Janen?"

Aldis acknowledged him with a slight tilt of his head. "Eylnen, it is good to see you."

"I wish I could say the same." Elinor shot him a look, but Con did not look in her direction. "The bodies of the Ninety-Fifth lay in a field outside this village. Their murderers are tucked safely away behind the walls of Height's Ward Keep, the keep you were charged with dismantling over a month ago. So, I say again, Janen, what has happened here?"

Aldis met his gaze. When he spoke, his words were heavy with bitterness. "I made a mistake," he said, his head drooping. "My duty was to pass the stewardship of the march to Lord Desmond, but I found an heir to the line of Redmayne. Garett is the youngest son, legitimate by blood, so I passed the line to him.

"Two days ago, Lord Desmond came to dispute the claim. Garett cut him down in the middle of the great hall like the bloodthirsty, hot-tempered little shit that he is." He gave a sad, despairing laugh. "And in that moment of murder, I lost everything. My honor. My pride. My men."

"Garett was not the rightful heir," Elinor said as a numb, cold feeling slowly spread from her stomach.

"What, Ellie?" Aldis asked.

"Lord Redmayne disowned him. It was public knowledge through the march. Desmond knew it, the villagers here knew it, and before you deny that you knew, Aldis, Warden Rollon would have known before he sent you out for the reaping." Disbelief and confusion warred within her as she locked eyes with him. "What the hell is really going on here?"

Aldis opened his mouth to speak, but no words came out.

The silence was utterly damning.

Con stared open-mouthed. "You made some kind of arrangement, didn't you? With Garett. You acknowledge him in exchange for something. What? Gold? Favors?"

"Oh how easy it must be for you to judge me from where you stand, Engineer."

"I stand here," Con said. "I stand exactly where your depravity has put us. Tell me I'm wrong." Con pointed at Elinor. "Tell her."

Aldis slowly raised his head toward Elinor. Silently, she watched him as his eyes sought hers and then quickly looked away.

"Oh, Aldis," she breathed.

"Don't look at me like that, Ellie. Not with those eyes. Not like I'm some monster from your old stories," Aldis said. "It all started with Warden Rollon. No, wait, Ellie, I'm not trying to transfer blame. You need to know how it works here. He controls everything in his domain. Everything flows through him here: gold, land, trade. And it all happens with a price, a price he sets. When Lord Redmayne died, there was an auction among lords, and Lord Desmond was the highest bidder. He paid the price to take over Cragswatch."

Aldis paced, wringing his hands. "I paid my dues as well. I wasn't assigned this duty. I paid the proper parties to ensure I got it. Reapers are treated well in Rollon's domain. By the new lords, by the people, by other lords who hope to gain our favor for future dealings. I knew I was going to be compensated far beyond what I spent to get it.

"But the night before we set forth to Cragswatch, Rollon himself called me in. He told me about Garett. Said that he would offer me a bribe to pass the line to him instead of Desmond. Rollon told me to accept it. Said that half of it was mine to keep.

"Rollon knew Desmond would come for his rightful claim, but said only one man could rule Cragswatch, and, in the end, they would settle it on their own. Both parties had already paid their dues, he said, and our part in it would be finished." Aldis stopped, burying his head in his hands.

Elinor wanted to turn away from him, but she kept her icy gaze fixed. "And you accepted."

"Rollon could have found any other officer to do this task and to turn him down would have meant the end of my career. Of everything."

"Your career, Aldis? Your—"

"I thought Garett was just some spoiled kid. I never thought he'd spill Desmond's blood in the grand hall and slaughter his entire retinue. And I never thought he would dare to strike a king's contingent." He shook his head over and over. "I was wrong, Ellie, so very wrong."

Elinor turned her head away from him, her eyes wet.

"Say something, Ellie," Aldis whispered.

No words came to her.

He took her hand. "You don't think I'm haunted by all those souls left in that clearing? That they won't haunt me the rest of my days? Don't you think I wish there was something I could do for those I left behind in Height's Ward?" As soon as the last words were out of his mouth, Aldis went silent.

Elinor's eyes sharpened to blue ice. "There are others alive in Height's Ward?" she whispered. "Survivors from the Ninety-Fifth?"

When he did not respond, her voice cracked out in the cold air, "Aldis! Are there soldiers of the Ninety-Fifth Pioneers still alive in that keep?"

Aldis put up his hands. "Elinor, don't be foolish. I know you. You cannot just go charging in there. Let's get back to the warden. We can convince him to help us. We can come back and bargain for the Ninety-Fifth."

"Don't you understand? Once we leave here and Garett knows we have escaped, he will not bother keeping hostages. If what you say about Warden Rollon is true, that he has washed his hands clean of this, then Garett will know those hostages have no value for him. The warden will not come to rescue these men and the army cannot move without the warden. Nobody is coming." She stared into his eyes. "Once we leave here, your men in the keep are as dead as the ones you failed out in that field."

"Petnar!" she called and the small, baldheaded man appeared immediately. "You will take Lieutenant Aldis Janen into custody for accepting bribes, dereliction of the sacred trust of his duty to the crown, and complicity in the deaths of soldiers of the King's Army."

Aldis did not resist as he stepped over and offered his hands to the befuddled engineer. "I never meant for this to happen," he said weakly.

Elinor was silent as he was led away.

She stared back at the keep for a long moment before feeling Con move up behind her.

"What are we going to do, Elinor?"

By the Ascended, she was tired, but her mind whirled with thought. Aldis was right. She could not face an enemy force that large. Even if she could, she could not ask her men to risk their lives for this.

But if they ran, she would be condemning those men inside to their deaths, and given Garett's rage, it would not be an easy one. Those men would suffer greatly before they died.

"Elinor?" Con asked again.

"See to the preparations to get our men out of here. That plan hasn't changed."

Con exhaled. "And you?"

"I just can't leave those men behind, Con."

"And what the hell do you plan to do?"

She offered him a halfhearted smile. "I'm sure I'll think of something."

Her attempt at humor did not seem to faze him. "Then we will stand with you," Con said, quietly resolute.

Elinor shook her head. "I cannot ask these men to stay behind."

"Yes, you can," Con urged. "You have to if you—"

"Con, enough, that is an order." It was harsher than she intended, but things were too dire now to mince words.

Con nodded then slowly walked away, leaving her alone.

Con

That damned Aldis Janen.

At the Academy, Con had always thought Aldis Janen associated with Elinor more for the rebellious thrill than any real loyalty and she had spent no small amount of time and energy getting him out of trouble. Now, it was the same thing.

Only this time, his trouble was going to get her killed.

"The prisoner has been secured, sir." Petnar's eyes were wide and his movements were sudden and jerky as he gave Con a nervous salute.

Con nodded. "Pet, I am going to need you to get the engineers prepped and ready to move on the hop. Now where is—" Before he could finish the thought, he saw Edmur approaching. "I was about to go track you down, Edmur."

"Figured as much," the foreman said. "So, you putting Petnar here in charge, Chief?"

"What?" Petnar asked.

Edmur gestured back to the town below. "You aim to go with the boss, right?"

Once again, Con was surprised at how perceptive the wily little foreman was. "There are soldiers of the King's Army in that keep," Con said. "She won't just walk away from this and leave their fates to that bastard Garett, especially not after he realizes that he's been duped."

"And you're truly going with her?" Petnar's mouth was agape. "Not transferring out is one thing, sir, but following her to your certain death is something else entirely."

"You know she's crazy, right?" Edmur asked with a laugh.

Con smiled. "I may have had the thought from time to time, but it's never stopped me, or her, before."

Edmur nodded. "That's why I didn't lead my crew out when the rest took off. Because of the boss. Who she is."

Petnar looked at the stout foreman. "I didn't figure you for being much on philosophical morality, Edmur."

"Oh, I follow the only philosophy that matters. Stay alive."

Petnar's eyes narrowed. "And you chose to stay with her after what happened in Timberline?"

Edmur's smile grew even wider. "Lotta bosses Lowside. Good ones, bad ones, murderous ones, take your pick, but trouble is gonna find you, no matter what you do. So you don't pick who to follow based on who will avoid trouble. You pick your poison on their ability to weather trouble when it comes and, the boss, she's tough. Purest brass as any I've ever seen."

"So you mean to stick around then?"

"Still decidin'" he said with a grin.

Con nodded. "The first day I met her, she did something that I thought... that everyone thought was impossible." Con paused, smiling at the memory. "She saved my life that day and walked out of a field of drowning grass with the jaw-bones of two rendworms."

"We've heard the tale," Petnar said. "Everybody knows the tale. It's what made her famous at the Academy."

Con shook his head. "It's what put a target on her back. She knew it and did it anyway. You just graduated, Pet. You don't know what the Academy was like before Elinor. It was the domain of the spoiled and the cruel, the children of nobles who had no other avenue to power. The Academy was their personal kingdom. As engineers, we went there to build things, Pet. They were there to break them."

Con rubbed a hand across his tired face. He remembered the mad dash into the drowning grass to rescue her from the rendworms and how in those days and months and years after, he joined her in that crusade at the Academy. The memory filled him with fierce pride.

"I didn't do a single important thing in my life until I met her," he said quietly. "I'm not about to miss out on this." As he spoke, Con's tension faded. He turned to Petnar and Edmur and grinned. "Are you?"

ALDIS

Elinor stepped inside, her face tight, but her blue eyes soft. "What happened to you, Aldis? You were a good man once."

Aldis sat on the straw-covered ground, his knees pulled up. "No, I wasn't. I never was." He idly played with a long piece of straw. "I was good to you, Ellie. There's a difference."

"Not to me, there isn't."

He stared at her. She had always been beautiful, but never like this. Years spent doing grunt work in the far marches and she actually looked better than at the Academy.

Only Elinor, only she could have stayed that way, while the rest of them had diminished.

Regret gripped him. Regret that he had been too much of a coward then to act on his feelings for her. And now, after everything he had become, regret turned to shame. He squeezed his eyes shut. "Don't do that. Don't make me feel worse than I already do right now."

"I am not here to make you feel worse. I am here because I need your help. You've been in that keep. You know where our people are being kept, where the sentries are—"

"No," he interrupted, shaking his head vehemently. "No, no, no. I'm not going to help you get yourself killed. Not you, Ellie, and especially not over something that's my fault. I've done a thousand foul things in my life, but I won't do that."

"Damn it, Aldis. This isn't about you."

"No, it isn't," he agreed. "It's about you. I don't care what happens to me now. I'll get what is coming to me, but I won't see you dead for my sins." He leaned toward her. "Get the hell out while you can."

"And leave those men and women to their fate?"

His stomach lurched and he fought the shame of it, but he would not lie to her. "Yes," Aldis said. "If it means no one else will suffer because of what has happened, then yes, damn it. I will live with that stain, that guilt, but I can't add the lives of you and your people to my list of sins. Please, just walk away from this."

Elinor held still. "You know I can't."

Aldis blew out an explosive breath in exasperation. "Damn your idealism, Elinor."

"It isn't idealism."

"The hell it isn't," Aldis fired back. "You just don't know…" he paused and calmed himself enough to lower his voice. "I wish I could still see the world like you do," he said, "like I did back the Academy, but that was all a lie. Those stories and traditions were just things they used to keep us in line. Everything's broken, Ellie."

Looking into her eyes, he deflated. "Everything but you," he said softly. "Unbent, unbroken, I wish I could be that way, but I have never been the man you imagined I was."

Elinor's face softened and she knelt beside him. "And I have never been that woman," she said. "You don't think I have doubts, Aldis? Fear? I do. I spent the last two years letting them rule me, but no more. Those stories and traditions, Aldis, are no lies. They are everything that truly matters and, one day, I will show you that."

Confused, Aldis stared at her. There was something about her, something powerful. Something that made her words ring like truth.

She held his focus. "In the Academy, we didn't fight for principles. We fought for each other. For Lida, and Con, and the others. We fought for you, Aldis, and you fought for us and no matter how broken everything may seem, that has never changed."

He tried to look away, but she touched his cheek, turning him back to her. "That is why I have to go back for those soldiers. They are our brothers and sisters, Aldis. This isn't about the warden. This is about us and them."

Slowly, she stood and adjusted the sword on her hip. "But I can't do this alone. We've always been stronger together, Aldis. I need you to help me do this."

Aldis looked up.

Damn her. There was always something about her that he could never walk away from, even when he knew it was a fool's wager. "So you want to end up a martyr, Elinor?"

At that, she smiled for the first time since she had stepped inside. "There are worse ends and, besides, they have to kill me first."

He smiled back for a moment and then shook his head forcefully. "How do you do that? How is it you always find a way to make me believe what you're talking about? That what you're proposing is anything other than pure madness and sure death?"

She met his gaze, blue eyes shining. "Because I believe in it," she said, taking his hand in hers. "Now, believe in me, like I believed in you."

ELINOR

Elinor walked out of the stable with Aldis behind her. His hands were unbound and he stood tall, following in her wake as she made her way up the hill.

Con waited with his arms crossed. He looked at Aldis and then back to Elinor, giving her a brief nod. Around him, Petnar, Edmur, and the rest of her engineers and workers arrayed themselves. Beside them, Oltan, the young man from the village, stood at the head of a group of a dozen villagers. They held farm implements and makeshift weapons.

Oltan crossed over to her. "My father was not cowed by Garett and neither will we be," he said. "Chief Eylnen has said you need help. We will stand with you, Lieutenant."

Elinor looked at Con with a raised eyebrow.

"I have been talking with Petnar and Edmur," Con said. "Then they got to talking with their people. Whatever you're planning, we are all with you."

She took a moment to look around at the assembled faces. Villagers, workers, engineers, all of them stared back at her, eyes filled with desperate intensity. She nodded slowly, pieces of plans and desperate gambits sliding into place.

Con gave her a worried look. "You do have something planned, right?"

"I do now."

She saw relief in his eyes as he rubbed his chin. "All right," he said, voice pitched loud. "So we can't defeat that force on the field and we can't take the keep. So what are we going to do, Lieutenant?"

Elinor looked over the crowd before turning back to Con, a smile breaking across her face. "First, we're going to defeat that force on the field, Journeyman Engineer, and then we're going to take that keep."

ELINOR

They made the ascent in the glow of moonlight.

Even with Oltan and his friends leading the troop, it had been slow going. Everything was cold stone and glittering ice, and the paths up the mountain were precarious.

Despite her earlier words of confidence, Elinor was no fool. Come morning, once Garett saw her force, small and on the run, he would come for her. She knew all too well that what was to come was going to be a bloody and difficult fight. The numbers were not on her side, that much was certain. She had a dozen engineers, the remnants of Edmur's work crew, and the young men and women from the village. All told, she could boast a force of just thirty swords, up against perhaps four times that number.

Worse, there were two Razors.

Those two alone could be a match for her group.

But Garett's force wasn't expecting a fight. They would come, ready for slaughter, the destruction of the Ninety-Fifth still fresh in their minds. They would come with Garett at their head, and that suited her fine. She had the measure of that man. She understood his temper and his cruelty. Just another bully, coming to collect his toll of pain.

Elinor was ready for him.

Oltan scrambled lightly over the rocks and dropped to the trail beside her. He was breathing quickly. "The place I told you of is just around the bend."

"Show me."

As they came around a turn, Elinor's eyes widened. Before her rose tall walls, sheathed in ice. They formed a narrow ravine, a scar cut into the stone of the mountain itself. No light from moon or stars could reach to the floor of the gorge and the small canyon was thick with darkness.

Elinor walked through it, walls making it feel like a tunnel of stone. The footing was slick and she had to reach out to steady herself.

"The snow and the ice here, they never melt," Oltan said quietly. "The walls are too high. They don't let in enough light, even in the summer months. Always, there is snow in the Scar of the Mountain."

Under her gloved hand, Elinor felt strange smooth grooves in the stone, like something had cut and carved away at the rock. She rubbed at it. "What did this?"

Oltan ran a hand along the smooth, worn grooves. "In the ancient days, there was a great battle here. One of the Ruins was cast down in defeat by the First Ascended, and the force of his fall carved the Scar."

Elinor rubbed her hand over the surface and smiled. "It is a well-chosen place, Oltan," she said. Elinor cast her eyes to the tops of the icy walls. "And you say you can get men up on top there?"

The young man nodded. "There are only two ways up the mountain. The Scar and the path across the top." He pointed up where she was looking.

"Perfect," Elinor said.

Two ways up, both highly defensible. Both terrible for horses.

This could be held.

Elinor issued orders. She sent a team of engineers with Petnar into the high path, overlooking the mouth of the ravine. They began to arrange rocks and deadfalls that could be triggered on the approach of Garett's force. The rest of her group went deep into the gorge and began construction on barricades and traps.

They worked through the remaining hours of the night, but, all too soon, the sky lightened. The first rays of sun crested the horizon, shining toward her.

"To your places!" Elinor commanded in a strong, clear voice.

A group of workers ran over to the cliff face. They pulled out metal shields and bits of armor that flashed brightly in the rising sun.

Elinor watched the keep, her teeth working at her lower lip as moments crawled by. Then she saw what she was waiting for: the gates of the keep opened and a large force of horsemen rode out, making directly for the base of the mountain.

Her thoughts went to Con, Aldis, and the group they were about to lead into that keep. She had drawn Garett's forces out. Now, it was in their hands.

No matter how much Elinor and her group fought, even if they somehow managed to rout Garett's forces, it would not matter if the keep was not taken. Garett could return to the safety of his walls and all would be lost. The survivors of the Ninety-Fifth would be dead, as would Con, Aldis, and the rest of the her troop.

All those who fell here would have died for nothing.

She shook her thoughts free with a grim smile. Hope was for the faithless. She knew that Con and Aldis would do their part.

She would do her part as well.

Elinor turned away from the precipice and prepared for the battle to come.

Con

In the gray predawn light, Height's Ward Keep towered above Con, but he was not looking at the keep. His eyes were on Aldis Janen.

"I can feel your eyes burning a hole in the back of my skull, Eylnen," Aldis said without turning around.

"Just waiting for you to run, Janen."

"If I was going to run, do you not think I would choose a more advantageous location than right here, at the very base of the keep?"

Before Con could retort, Edmur's face peered over the edge. He pulled down the scarf covering his face. "Ta, sirs. I hate to interrupt this strategic meeting of the king's finest, but you two are louder than a Prionside whore with a gold piece on her nightstand. Mind keeping it down so you don't draw any attention to our skullduggery?"

Chastised, Con closed his mouth and resumed waiting.

Edmur had brought three members of his work crew. The two he referred to as "the twins" were brothers absolutely identical in appearance. They had not spoken a single word the whole way out, instead communicating with each other using strange gestures.

The final member of the detail was a barrel-chested man called Iron Tosh. Con had seen him on past jobs, bracing the big winches they used to take down walls with just his own massive arms. Right now, Con could hear him working away with a pry bar against the grating that blocked the drainage run.

Then, in the cold morning air, he heard the sharp, grating sound of the keep's heavy gates opening. The ground shook with the force of galloping horsemen as they rode off toward the mountain, toward Elinor.

The attack was beginning.

Con moved to join the others. "They're on the move. Our time is now," he whispered.

Edmur nodded. "You heard the man, Tosh. Quit the gentle stuff and put it to the hop."

There was a groaning of steel as the grating bent. Con froze, his hand on the hilt of his sword as he waited for alarmed shouts from within the keep, but there was nothing.

They moved into the opening and Con breathed a small sigh.

"We need the prisoners," Con said, reiterating the plan. "We free the prisoners, take the keep from the inside, and let the lieutenant work out the rest." Getting his bearings, Con spotted a stone stairwell. He felt a hand on his shoulder before he reached it.

"We need to go this way," Aldis said, gesturing with his chin in the direction of an arched passage.

Con roughly shrugged the hand off his shoulder. "I know the construction of keeps like this. I got us to the wash grate that got us inside and I know that these stairs will take us down into the lower levels to where the dungeon should be."

"Should be?" Aldis said. "Eylnen, I was held in this keep. I know where the dungeon is. The lower levels are huge. I heard them talking about the storehouses that are built down there. Your way will cost us time we do not have." He pointed toward a large tunnel. "We go that way. It opens up into the courtyard. The prisoners are being held on the other side."

"You want us to cross the open courtyard?" Con asked incredulously. "If Garett left anyone behind, they'll be there and we'll run right into them before we make it across the courtyard."

"Then we deal with them. I know Garett. He will put almost everything into the attack. A threat to the keep is something he cannot fathom. He has taken what he sees as his birthright. No one would dare intrude inside it."

Faint, indistinct sounds drifted through the opening in the wall behind them. Garett's force had reached Elinor at the mountain. The fight was on.

"We have no time, Eylnen," Aldis said and gave a tight-lipped smile. "Trust me, Conbert."

Con grimaced. "That was the last thing you should have said to me."

"Then trust Elinor."

Con growled in frustration, but said, "Fine," and then, they were moving, following Aldis through the arched tunnel.

They took a few quick twists and turns before exiting into the open courtyard. The sun was just cresting the horizon, filling the sky with red rays.

Aldis motioned them back against the wall as they inched their way around the courtyard. They came to a heavy door and slipped inside, quiet as ghosts as they descended the steps beyond.

As Con came to the bottom floor, he saw the twins standing over a crumpled body. Beyond, the room had three doors. The twins pointed to one and Con moved to it, pulling back a panel to look inside. The room was pitch black.

"Ninety-Fifth Pioneers," Con whispered fiercely. "At the ready!" He spoke the soldier's call to attention and hoped for a response from the blackness.

Slowly, a woman's face came into view, emerging from the darkness. One of her eyes was swollen shut and she hobbled with a noticeable limp. Her eyes were cold and hard. "Stand and declare," she whispered back.

"Journeyman Engineer Conbert Eylnen, Chief of Engineers under Lieutenant Elinor. We're here to get you out."

At his words, there were muffled whispers from the darkness behind her, but she motioned for silence. "Sergeant Kyra of the Ninety-Fifth. Glad to see you, sir," she said. "We stand ready." Her voice was even, but her eyes were wet.

Edmur rifled loudly through the corpse's pockets, shaking his head after drawing Con's attention. "No key, Chief." He gestured to Iron Tosh. "Not to worry. We'll have that door open like a brothel at midnight. Just a few ticks."

Metal scraped on metal as they worked.

Con looked up and met Aldis's gaze. The other man was quiet.

Behind Aldis, the third door opened.

Three men came into the prison chamber talking and laughing. They froze as they came face to face with Aldis.

Aldis punched the nearest one in the face, and everyone sprang into motion.

One man grabbed Aldis, pulling both of them down. The other drew his sword with a snarl and rushed forward to attack. The twins met him, sharp blades suddenly appearing in their hands.

The third man ran.

Con drew his own sword and lunged for the fleeing man. The scuffling duo of Aldis and his opponent rolled around between Con and the doorway, costing him precious seconds. By the time he reached the door, the man was already turning a corner and disappearing from view.

Then, just a moment later, a bell began tolling.

"Edmur!" Con shouted. "They sounded the alarm!"

"You don't say," Edmur snapped.

He and Iron Tosh gave up subtlety and began pounding away at the iron lock. The twins finished off their man and helped Aldis deal with his.

The sounds of footsteps echoed through the door above.

"They're here!" Aldis yelled. "Edmur! We need reinforcements right now!"

Bright light entered the room as the door at the top of the stairs opened. Aldis charged up, catching the first bandit through with a well-placed thrust.

Con took a step back, his officer's sword ready. One of the twins had moved up the stairs to help.

"Give, you bastard!" Edmur shouted.

There was a ringing sound as the cell door popped open. Weary and injured soldiers wearing the black and silver of the King's Own poured into the room. Sergeant Kyra moved quickly, delivering weapons from the ground to her fellow soldiers.

Garett's bandits flooded in. All was chaos as pressing bodies filled the small room. There was barely space to swing a sword. Con thrust with the ornate hilt of his blade, smashing it into any unfamiliar face.

In the mad press, Con was shoved back and forth while fighting and jabbing at any enemy. He pulled up at the sight of the familiar black army uniform in front of him, unsure if he was glad he had managed to stop the blow.

It was Aldis Janen.

Aldis leaned closer to him. "The banner!" he yelled.

Con frowned in confusion, pushing a bandit away. "What?" he yelled over the din.

"The banner!" Aldis repeated. "We have to get the banner up or Elinor will have no chance." He gestured toward the sunlight-framed doorway at the top of the stairs, blocked by Garett's soldiers. "You with me, Eylnen?"

Con wanted to call him a traitor, wanted to tell him to go to hell, but he could not argue that Aldis was right. They had to get the banner up and convince that bastard Garett his keep was lost. Without that, Elinor would not be able to withstand his attack for long.

Con nodded once and they were moving. Aldis and Con were not fighting to kill now, only to get out. One man slashed at Aldis, who parried and stepped aside as Con grabbed the man by his belt, pulling him off balance and sending him off the stairs. Shadows came at them, but fortunately Aldis was quick enough with his blade to strike them before they could slow.

Then they were out into the blinding morning sunlight. Con struggled to adjust his vision, focusing on keeping pace with Aldis's sprint.

They made it together to the tall central tower's barbican.

As Con entered the tower archway, something slammed into his right shoulder, sending him reeling. He crashed against the wall, an arrow protruding from him. A quick hand dragged him around the wall as another arrow struck the stone where he had been.

It was hard for him to take a full breath and he slumped down to the ground, gasping for air. Over the sound of his own ragged breathing, he became aware of a voice calling to him.

"Eylnen. Eylnen! Con!"

He opened his eyes. Aldis leaned over him. Gritting his teeth against the pain, Con reached inside his officer's jacket and produced the banner of the Ninety-Fifth. The black fabric glistened wetly, and Con knew it was from his blood.

He shoved the banner into the hands of its former commander. "Do it," he said through gritted teeth. "Do not fail her again, Aldis."

Aldis's fingers tightened on the banner as he pulled it free. "I won't," he said.

Con watched as Aldis, sword in one hand, banner in the other, moved around the corner to charge the stairs. Before he went unconscious, the last sounds Con heard were Aldis's defiant yell and the snap of a bowstring.

ELINOR

Garett's forces thundered up the mountain pass.

As they flew around the final bend, their rapid advance was stopped by broken wagons blocking the path. The lead horsemen hit the icy ground when they forced their mounts around. Horses slipped and skidded into each other and the advance faltered.

Elinor slashed her sword through the air and men in the higher ground released the first of the deadfalls.

The side of the mountain shook with the thunder of rolling boulders. The rocks crashed against the vanguard of Garett's fighters. Horses frantically reared and scrambled, their hooves sliding on ice, many going down hard. The beasts slid onto their sides, sending riders screaming over the cliff edge.

Amidst the chaos, Garett's men dismounted and scrambled up the path toward Elinor.

"To me!" Elinor shouted. "For the King and the Ninety-Fifth!"

From the darkened shadows of the ravine, her men and women surged forth, choking the narrow entrance.

Elinor rushed toward the first soldier, and chaos and cacophony enveloped her. Despite the screaming faces and flashing steel, she was aware enough to know the line was holding. At least for now.

Elinor cleared space, driving back Garett's men. "The ballista! Now!"

The ballista's thrumming string was immediately overshadowed by a forceful bolt slamming into an enemy. It took him off his feet and continued unabated into the crowd of soldiers.

Elinor stared with grim satisfaction.

A commotion in the heights above drew her attention and her stomach dropped.

On the higher path, Petnar was on his knees, weakly swinging his sword. His face was streaked with blood. Some of his fellow engineers were down as well, while others remained fighting as Garett's men flowed up the path. For a brief moment, Petnar locked eyes with her and she saw pain and regret.

Then, he was lost behind rushing soldiers.

She was about to be flanked. Garett's force would flow into the deeper part of the ravine behind them and flush her small group out to be cut to ribbons.

"Oltan!" Elinor called out.

The young man turned her way. Oltan's face was streaked with blood, but his eyes were wide and alert.

"Oltan, hold them here. You have to hold them," Elinor said and darted back into the ravine.

She sprinted down the gorge, the snow and ice slick under foot, the sheer walls blurring as she ran. She came to the higher path just as the first of the bandit force was coming around the craggy rocks of the mountain face.

Elinor slashed with her sword, cutting the first man down. She lowered her shoulder and smashed the shining, steel pauldron on her left shoulder into the face of the next man. Elinor heard bones break and she tossed him out of her way, trying to reach the next man.

As she fought, she heard a woman's voice call out, "Ignore her! Take the gorge and wipe them out."

Elinor caught sight of the woman. She wore her long, black hair in a tightly coiled braid, and she gestured with a long-bladed knife in either hand. The woman met Elinor's gaze and smiled.

Razor, Elinor thought. *Damn.*

Elinor cut viciously with her sword, forcing her nearest opponents back and buying herself more space. She pushed sideways and dropped to her knees before kicking her legs out and sending herself sliding down the tall rocks lining the path.

She slid along the ice-covered stone and over the lip of the wall. Using the pommel of her sword to slow her descent, she dug into ice. Even with that, she landed hard on the ravine's cold ground, the impact stealing breath from her lungs.

Elinor leaped up, turning to meet the first of the bandits coming into the gorge. She took the surprised man with a high thrust, sending him screaming to the ground. Elinor forced her body forward, crowding into the next man, denying him room to use his long-handled axe. She struck her pommel into the bandit's face, and he crumpled under the assault.

The pounding of running feet caused her to look up. A huge figure with a large hammer barreled down the trail at her. The air around him seemed to be sucked into his path, crackling with energy.

The huge man smashed into Elinor, his already powerful force augmented. The world exploded in bright light as she flew across the width of the gorge. Elinor crashed into the far wall, the impact shattering ice. Her vision graying, Elinor slumped to one knee, fighting to draw breath.

Through her blurred vision, she caught a glimpse of movement coming over the ice wall. The woman with the long, black braid leapt across the gorge. With both arms extended, the dark-haired woman slid down the ice and then, with an impossible grace, flipped off the wall.

Elinor raised her sword as the woman landed directly in front of her. Elinor cut, but the Razor bent backwards, allowing the slash to pass harmlessly, and dropped into a spin. Elinor felt a cold sensation in her stomach, and she looked down.

The hilt of the Razor's blade stuck from her midsection.

There wasn't pain, but her limbs were heavy and numb. Elinor tried to raise her sword, but her arm was leaden. She staggered back and pulled at the blade in her belly. It came free covered in dark, red blood.

Her knees buckled, dropping her to the icy ground. Kneeling, breath coming fast and shallow, Elinor saw the huge, hammer-wielding Razor move beside the woman as bandits swarmed from the trail.

Head spinning, breath ragged, Elinor dropped her sword from numb fingers. Slowly, her hands clenched into tight fists. All the sound in her world faded and she heard her heart's rhythmic beating.

Deep within the mountain, something answered that sound.

Low and powerful, a sound came to her. A deep, solid groaning, as if the bones of the earth itself were stirring.

The Razor with the knife approached her, murder in her eyes.

Elinor closed her eyes and slammed her clenched fists to the ground. Along the length of the ravine, ice shattered like glass.

Above her, where bandits were flowing into the gorge, rocks dislodged, hurling Garett's men screaming from the ledge. Boulders cracked and fell, smashing onto the battle below. Screams of confusion and panic filled the air.

Beneath it, the hum of the earth filled her, resonating within her.

Elinor drew strength from it, enough to lift her sword. Blade in one hand, the Razor's knife in the other, Elinor rose.

The Razor reversed her grip on her remaining knife. She slashed out at Elinor's eyes. It was a quick cut, but Elinor knocked it aside. The force of the deflection caught the Razor by surprise, throwing her off balance. Elinor stabbed the short blade into the woman's exposed side, felling her.

The Razor with the hammer charged again. Elinor swung her sword savagely, her limbs driven with a strength she had never known before. The blade struck the metal head of the hammer with a ringing peal like a bell, and the hammer shattered. Bits of metal sprayed into the Razor's face and he screamed. Elinor's second blow cut the screaming abruptly off.

The deep sound from within the mountain began to fade, and with it, Elinor felt her newfound strength fading. Pain and weakness flowed into her and she stumbled.

As chaos returned to her ears, a panicked call for retreat sounded behind Elinor. She looked down the length of the gorge and saw Garett waving a sword in the air.

He was pulling his soldiers back.

No, Elinor thought. *Not now. Not with him so close.* But it was no use. She could see the fear on the would-be lord's face. He would turn and lead his still sizeable force back to the keep to lick his wounds in safety.

Elinor saw Oltan spring atop one of the fallen boulders and point into the land below. "The banner!" the young man yelled. "The banner flies! The keep has been taken!"

Confusion and chaos spread through Garett's force like a brush fire through dry grass. There was no orderly withdrawal now. Bandits fled from the ravine, moving past the trail's wagon-strewn entrance in singles and pairs, abandoning the fight.

Her strength fading, the pain beginning to fill her, Elinor ran.

Her legs pumped and her arms swung while the sword and knife gleamed. Lungs burning and head swimming, Elinor ran past her soldiers and the enemy fighters, eyes never straying from her quarry. She mounted a large rock with a lunging step and then leaped.

Garett Redmayne looked up just as Elinor descended upon him. The look of shock was still in his eyes as his head flew from his body.

She landed hard, without strength left to catch herself. Snow and ice covered her face from the impact and she pulled herself up slowly. Around her, broken and panicked remnants of Garett's force continued their flight.

Cheers from her small, valiant band echoed from the mountain heights, and from the trail head, engineers from the upper path carried down their wounded and their dead. She thought she saw Petnar being helped along.

As she sat slumped in the snow, leaning on her blade, she looked down from the side of the mountain into the land below.

Slowly, she smiled.

Even from here, she saw the tattered banner of the Ninety-Fifth Pioneers flying high over Height's Ward Keep.

CON

Con sat in a rough wooden chair outside one of the village houses. His shoulder ached with a dull throb and the coarse, fabric bandages were stained with blood.

But he was alive.

All around, villagers mingled with the survivors from the Ninety-Fifth who had been freed from the keep, laughing and celebrating.

Edmur walked over, a bottle of wine in his hand. He extended it to Con, who took the bottle and drank. The wine was rich and sweet.

Con offered the bottle back to Edmur, but the foreman refused. "Nah, Chief. You get that down. You need it more than I do." He turned and walked away. "Besides, I ain't getting caught with that. You army types are awful strict. They hang looters, you know."

Con spit out wine. "Looters?"

Edmur walked into the crowd, a wide grin on his face.

"That's her coming now." Aldis's voice caused Con to turn suddenly and the wound in his shoulder twinged in protest.

Con gritted his teeth to keep from crying out. "You mind not sneaking up on an injured man?"

Aldis came up next to Con's chair and they stared across the plain to where Elinor's group was slowly coming toward them.

"You know, an engineer with your knowledge of mechanics and the physical world and such should have enough sense to know to duck," Aldis commented.

A dozen retorts came to Con's mind. Foremost among them was the idea that perhaps Aldis Janen was too good at ducking and needed to learn how to stand. In light of the victory, and the fact that Aldis had saved his life a number of times in the mad dash to the banner, Con held his tongue. *Elinor would have approved of that, he thought.*

"Wine, Janen?" he asked and offered the bottle to Aldis, who accepted it and drank thirstily.

"This is delightful," he said with a look of surprise.

"Keep the bottle," Con said with a wave of his hand and hid his smile.

As the train of men and women drew closer, Aldis shook his head. "Every time I doubt her, she proves me wrong, Eylnen. Every time."

In the man's voice, Con heard pain and shame. His anger at Aldis was far from faded, but he knew that Aldis had much to answer for from the King's Army and the warden. He could have run, probably should have run, but Aldis was still here. That softened Con toward him a bit.

"Then do what I have done, Janen. Stop doubting her."

The two looked on in silence as Elinor drew nearer. Her face was solemn and drawn, and she rode slowly along the column. Behind her, one of the wagons carried a small stack of wrapped bodies. After that came the engineers, villagers, and the rest of Edmur's work crew.

As the villagers saw their loved ones returning, they ran out to meet them. The air was abuzz with greetings and shared tales.

Elinor dismounted and made her way over. Her eyes went to Con's wounded shoulder, and she hastened forward the last few steps, concern on her face.

Before she could speak, Con raised a finger. "See? Now you know how I felt all those times I came back and had to patch you up." He paused. "And it looks like this time is no exception," he said, spying the wrapping of bandages peeking out from under her black uniform.

Elinor laughed, though her eyes showed exhaustion. "Point taken," she said and leaned forward to embrace him. "You did good."

Con was careful with his embrace, not wanting to aggravate her wounds, but his heart swelled.

Aldis gave her a tilt of his head, and asked, "Surprised to see me?"

"No," Elinor said. "I knew you would be here, but you know you still have much to answer for, Aldis."

"I do," he said. "That's what makes this so necessary." He undid the clasps of his scabbard and then laid his sheathed sword across the backs of his closed fists, surrendering the blade to Elinor. "In light of the accusations leveled against me, I am suspending my commission. You are acting commander of the Ninety-Fifth Pioneers now, Elinor."

"Aldis…" she started.

He shook his head. "They won't follow me now, Ellie. Not after what happened. Nor should they. But they all know what you did for them. They will follow you."

Con smiled at her. "Ninety-Fifth Pioneers!" he called out, his voice loud enough to carry over the sound of the celebration. It hurt his wound a bit, but the look on her face with what came next was worth the pain.

Wherever they were, members of the Ninety-Fifth immediately snapped to attention, their right fists pressed over their hearts. All of them saluting their new commander.

"Well, Lieutenant?" Aldis asked, his grin returned. "What are your orders?"

All those assembled looked to her expectantly.

For a brief moment, Con saw a wide smile before she pointed at Aldis. "See to establishing a perimeter and start patrols in case the remains of Garett's forces attempt to regroup without him and return.

"Oltan, I need you to coordinate with a group of soldiers that I will select and guide them to Lord Desmond's march. We need to let his heir know what has transpired here.

"Petnar, send a dispatch to Army Command in Resa detailing these events. Have it ready within the hour."

Petnar saluted smartly.

"Edmur, get your people together and figure out how many bodies you will need to supplement the work crews. You start unloading the wagons tomorrow. We are going to finish the original task of the Ninety-Fifth."

In the wake of her orders, people moved quick. As she watched, Con slowly got to his feet. It was difficult and for a moment he was a little lightheaded, but he steadied himself.

Elinor turned, opening her mouth to speak, but then paused and looked back toward the men and women around them. "Once things are settled here, I will present the Ninety-Fifth to the warden. After that, we need to return to Timberline." There was intensity in her eyes and voice.

"Timberline? Elinor, what is going on?"

Elinor stared off toward the mountains. She spoke with a hushed voice only they could hear. "Something happened up there, Con. Something that I believe only the Shepherd can answer."

"Something?" Con's eyes were wide as he moved closer. "Something what?"

"I don't know," Elinor said before smiling. "Something good."

ALDIS

The moonlight caught the swirl of frost on the tree branches, making them glitter like sharpened knives. Aldis Janen pulled his cloak closer about him and checked to make sure he was not being followed through the forest.

He pushed past the final trees and moved into a clearing. In the center, amidst the perfection of pristine white snow, a hooded figure was waiting for him.

The figure turned slowly, its face obscured by the heavy, hooded cloak it wore. Slowly, it pulled it back, revealing the thin face of Bayun, Warden Rollon's chamberlain.

Aldis raised his chin in an attempt at defiance. Even he felt how utterly unconvincing it was. For Bayun to have left the warden's side and come out here in person spoke volumes about how much this meeting meant. Aldis felt the weight of that around his neck like a hangman's noose. He choked that down and worked his tongue around his dry mouth to try and speak.

"I won't betray her," Aldis said.

Bayun extended his hands in a shrug-like gesture. "Then help us," Bayun whispered in a soft voice. "And it may not come to that."

The words carried across the clearing. Aldis felt his hands clenching and unclenching uncontrollably. He spoke at last, forcing his words through gritted teeth, "I do this, then I'm done."

"You have the warden's word. Now, listen and listen well."

Despite himself, Aldis Janen listened.

Follow the continuing stories of Elinor in Book 3.
Coming Soon.

ACKNOWLEDGMENTS

Mark: To my brother Dave, my wife Tiffany, and my son Bryce for their love and support. And to my mom and dad, Dan and Pam Gelineau, who I miss every day, and who made me everything I am.

Joe: To Irene, Emma, and Kate. Because of you, I know I can do, and be, anything. In every way that counts, these stories are for you.

A very special thanks to Jason. His beautiful work on our website, ebooks, and paperbacks has been inspiring, and his dogged editing and persistence has pushed us to become better on every level. But most of all, he believed in us, often times more than we believed in ourselves, and that is something that we will never forget or ever fully repay.

And a huge thank you to the rest of our insanely talented (and far too good for the likes of us) team.

Our editor, Susan at West of Mars, who always manages to find the heart of our stories. Our copy editor, TJ Redig, whose humor and skill keeps both us and our stories moving. And of course to Marija at Damonza, our cover designer, who blows us away every time she brings our characters and world to life.

Finally, to our supremely patient and forgiving beta readers: Maria, Emily, Samantha, Beth, Kevin, and Megan. Thank you, thank you, and thank you. We ask a lot of you, and we ask it a lot! But you are always there for us. We wouldn't be here without you.

Author's Note
Echoes of the Ascended, Books 2

We thought we knew what we were getting into.

We did not.

We were fools.

But after finishing this second round of books, we are grateful that we were and still remain foolish enough to keep our heads down and just keep moving forward.

It was a difficult year. Mark lost his father, after losing his mother only a year before. In many ways, it was because of Mark's mother that we even took these tentative first steps, and this past year, it was his father that inspired us every day to keep going.

He was a great man.

Thinking about our own families and all things said and unsaid, we both realized how much of our hearts are in our stories.

Our characters are brave and foolish and believe in things that perhaps they shouldn't. So did our parents. And one day, that is our hope for our children as well.

It's cheezy, it's sappy, but having kids will do that to you!

But that's us. Writers. Fathers. Fools.

Thank you for taking a chance on us and our stories and for coming along for the ride.

We'll see you again for books 3, out in a few months. Til then, we hope you too are foolish enough to keep chasing the things you love.

Mark & Joe

GELINEAU AND KING

Thank you for reading this Gelineau and King novella.

Visit us on the web at www.gelineauandking.com and join us on our mailing list for the latest releases, news, and promotions.

Like us at facebook.com/gelineauandking.

Follow us on Twitter @gelineauandking.

Or send us your best wishes via astral projection. Whatever your medium, we accept love in all its forms. Hope to see you again soon.

SKINSHAPER
REND THE DARK BOOK 2

PROLOGUE

PROLOGUE

THE CAGE SWUNG BACK AND forth in the icy wind above the deserted town. It dangled from a length of frost-covered chain, high above the buildings of the camp. Inside the iron bars, a woman held herself still. The sound came from far away, from inside the dark entrance of the mine. Her eyes narrowed and she held her breath, desperate to hear the sound once more. For a long moment, all that filled the air was the mournful howl of icy wind.

Then she heard it again.

Pounding feet.

She twisted in the narrow iron cage. Hope and horror warred within her as she held her breath and watched.

A figure broke free from the darkness of the mine and into the cold light of morning. He ran with a frantic intensity, arms and legs pumping. He shot across the bare white snow and into town. She watched with desperate, yearning hope as he ran through empty streets.

And then a chorus of gibbering shrieks sounded from the depths of the mine.

Hope shriveled and died inside her.

The man looked back and stumbled in the snow, falling forward onto his face. He scrambled to his feet, his face a mask of desperate terror.

From the mine, three twisted, broken shapes emerged.

They were fast, cavorting across the snow and ice with horrible, misshapen limbs. Too many legs and joints bending the wrong way. Arms with feet at the ends instead of hands. Madness made flesh.

The man pushed harder, his arms and legs flailing, but the creatures chased with impossible speed. The snow did not slow them. The ice did not cause them to slip or skitter out of control. They were made for the hunt and they descended upon him like wolves on a deer.

She shut her eyes as they dragged the screaming man back into the mine.

Then all was silent.

The woman didn't cry. She just sat still and waited for her turn to die.

A Reaper of Stone

A Lady is dead. Her noble line ended. And the King's Reaper has come to reclaim her land and her home. In the marches of Aedaron, only one thing is for certain. All keeps of the old world must fall.

Elinor struggles to find her place in the new world. She once dreamed of great things. Of becoming a hero in the ways of the old world. But now she is a Reaper. And her duty is clear. Destroy the old. Herald the new.

"A classic fantasy tale with a strong, admirable heroine and a nice emotional punch. Great start to an enjoyable new series!"
— RL King, author of *The Alastair Stone Chronicles*

"A Reaper of Stone has the essence of a traditional fantasy epic, full of adventure and beautiful, lyrical prose, in well under a hundred pages."
— *Books by Proxy*

Broken Banners
A Reaper of Stone book 2

Slaughtered and left for crows, soldiers of the King's Army lay dead in a field. A grim reminder: the king's law ends at the gates of the capital.

Elinor fought for what she believed and now she is an outcast. No soldier will follow her. No officer will stand with her. Yet when she finds her brothers and sisters slaughtered, she cannot turn her back on them.

Long ago, they swore an oath. Not to the king, but to each other.

And woe to those who break that bond.

"[A] short epic, full of hope and victory where none can be found... The world these authors created is unbelievably tangible."

– Twin Reads

Rend the Dark

The great Ruins are gone. The titans. The behemoths. All banished to the Dark and nearly forgotten. But the cunning ones, the patient ones remain. They hide not in the cracks of the earth or in the shadows of the world. But inside us. Wearing our skin. Waiting. Watching.

Once haunted by visions of the world beyond, Ferran now wields that power to hunt the very monsters that he once feared. He is not alone. Others bear the same terrible burden. But Hunter or hunted, it makes no difference. Eventually, everything returns to the Dark.

"Atmospheric, fast paced, engaging quick read, with a satisfying story and glimpses of Supernatural *and King's* IT.*"*

— *BooksChatter*

BEST LEFT IN THE SHADOWS

A Highside girl. Beaten. Murdered. Her body found on a Lowside dock. A magistrate comes looking for answers. For justice.

Alys trades and sells secrets among the gangs and factions of Lowside. She is a daughter of the underworld. Bold. Cunning. Free. When an old lover asks for help, she agrees. For a price.

Together, they travel into the dark heart of the underworld in search of a killer.

"I was blown away by the detail and world building that was accomplished in so few pages. I didn't feel like I was seeing a section of a puzzle, more like I was reading a story that would contribute to a larger whole, but is compelling and rich all on its own."

– Mama Reads, Hazel Sleeps

Faith and Moonlight

Roan and Kay are orphans.

A fire destroys their old life, but they have one chance to enter the School of Faith.

They are given one month to pass the entry trials, but as Roan excels and Kay fails, their devotion to each other is put to the test.

They swore they would face everything together, but when the stakes are losing the life they've always dreamed of, what will they do to stay together?

What won't they do?

"You can really feel Roan's desire and dream to be something more and you can also feel Kay's frustration and struggle. And underneath all that you can practically touch how much they care about each other."

– White Sky Project

33892141R00058

Made in the USA
San Bernardino, CA
27 April 2019